Punished by the Principal

BY

Annabelle Winters

Copyright Notice

Books by Annabelle Winters

The CURVES FOR SHEIKHS Series
Curves for the Sheikh
Flames for the Sheikh
Hostage for the Sheikh
Single for the Sheikh
Stockings for the Sheikh
Untouched for the Sheikh
Surrogate for the Sheikh
Stars for the Sheikh
Shelter for the Sheikh
Shared for the Sheikh
Assassin for the Sheikh
Privilege for the Sheikh
Ransomed for the Sheikh
Uncorked for the Sheikh
Haunted for the Sheikh
Grateful for the Sheikh
Mistletoe for the Sheikh
Fake for the Sheikh

The CURVES FOR SHIFTERS Series
Curves for the Dragon
Born for the Bear
Witch for the Wolf
Tamed for the Lion
Taken for the Tiger

The CURVY FOR HIM Series
The Teacher and the Trainer
The Librarian and the Cop
The Lawyer and the Cowboy
The Princess and the Pirate

The CEO and the Soldier
The Astronaut and the Alien
The Botanist and the Biker
The Psychic and the Senator

THE CURVY FOR THE HOLIDAYS SERIES

Taken on Thanksgiving
Captive for Christmas
Night Before New Year's
Vampire's Curvy Valentine
Flagged on the Fourth
Home for Halloween

THE CURVY FOR KEEPS SERIES

Summoned by the CEO
Given to the Groom
Traded to the Trucker
Punished by the Principal
Wifed by the Warlord

THE DRAGON'S CURVY MATE SERIES

Dragon's Curvy Assistant
Dragon's Curvy Banker
Dragon's Curvy Counselor
Dragon's Curvy Doctor
Dragon's Curvy Engineer
Dragon's Curvy Firefighter
Dragon's Curvy Gambler

THE CURVY IN COLLEGE SERIES

The Jock and the Genius
The Rockstar and the Recluse
The Dropout and the Debutante
The Player and the Princess
The Fratboy and the Feminist

WWW.ANNABELLEWINTERS.

Punished by the Principal

BY

Annabelle Winters

1
<u>RHODES</u>

"This isn't a military school, Rick."

"Call me Rick again. Go on. I dare you."

I stand up behind my desk, my knees hitting the tabletop from below. This desk belongs in a Lego Playset, not a grown man's office. Who the fuck was the previous Principal, anyway? An elf?

"Right. You aren't Rick no more," says Duff, grinning wide enough to show off that gap in his teeth from the night before he flamed out of bootcamp. "Principal Rhodes. Got a nice ring to it. Do you make the teachers call you Sir?"

I grunt at Duff, planting my fists on the table and leaning my weight forward. I feel the wood groan, and I press harder. Maybe if I break the desk I can order a new one. Though the tightwads on the School Board will probably replace it with a plastic folding table even though the coffers are overflowing, thanks to the demand for a spot in this school. They do pay the teachers and staff very well, I'll give them that. I'd have taken this job for a whole lot less money. Not that I'm complaining, of course—but I'm here for reasons other than cold hard cash.

"You got a reason for being here, Duff?" I stretch my arms out wide, flexing my shoulder blades and then cracking my neck. Sitting at a desk is murder on the muscles. I need to find a way to get a workout in during the day. Can't lose my edge just because I'm no longer in a war zone.

Though maybe this is a different sort of war zone, I think as Duff shifts on his feet and rubs the back of his neck. I know why he's here, and although I'd do anything for the brothers and sisters on my team, I can't help him out on this one. Besides, he only lasted a few weeks on my team—and that was just bootcamp. Bailed before we saw any action.

"C'mon, Rick—I mean Principal Rhodes," he says through that holey grin. "Do a brother a solid. My ex-wife's been hounding me to pull some strings and get the boy into your school."

I sigh and run my fingers through my hair that's short but still longer than it's ever been. Though before the military I had it down past my shoulders, I guess. Thank heavens for the military. Without that discipline I'd have probably turned into a beach bum with no ambitions other than banging sunburned chicks on the hot sands of Southern California.

"Firstly, this isn't *my* school," I say, glancing at the moonfaced clock on the dark green wall. "Secondly, that isn't even your kid! Your ex got remarried, knocked up, and now she's after you to pull some strings for the other guy's kid? What happened to your balls, Duff? Oh right. You never had any."

Duff clenches his jaw so hard he almost bites his tongue off, and I stare coolly at him like I'm daring him to stand up to me. I have unconditional love for anyone who fought with me, but Duff never stood with us on the field of battle. The military isn't for everyone, but Duff should have figured that out sooner. Having someone bail on his brothers and sisters affects morale, and low morale gets people killed.

Duff mutters something and looks down at the floor. Then he shakes his head and storms out of my office, slamming the door pointedly like an angry child. That round clock above the door shivers but stands its ground, and I sigh and stride over to straighten it.

But just as I reach up for it, the door swings open and almost clocks me in the face! I jump back like a jungle cat, every muscle coiled as I plant my feet into the floor and ready myself to fight to the death. I know it's just the years of training that's now part of my instinct, and I know I need to turn that shit down if I'm going to make a go of it in civilian life.

"Who are you? Where's Sally?" comes a woman's voice.

I stay in my crouching-tiger stance and tilt my head left while raising my right eyebrow. Without moving my eyeballs I take in the sight of the un-invited intruder. She's in a brown skirt-suit, fitted to perfection over curves that make my cock go on high alert like it's being ambushed. Pretty face round like that clock, lips like a red sunset, brown eyes sharp like spears, hair the color of rain-darkened earth, with long strands hanging loose past her shoulders, still slightly wet. Immediately I picture her in the shower this morning, naked just an hour ago perhaps, thick lather rolling down those hefty breasts, heavy foam gathering in that V between her thighs, no amount of lavender scent able to hide the feminine musk of her pussy from my hungry nostrils.

"Who the hell is Sally?" I say, swallowing hard as I feel a thickness in my throat, the blood already charging south of the border, filling out my off-the-rack gray suit-trousers to the point where I feel the cheap seams strain like they're going to give up the ghost.

"Um, she's the Principal?" says the woman, bobbing her head like I'm an idiot. "Who the hell are you? The janitor?"

I blink twice and twist the edge of my mouth. Then I straighten to full height and look down at myself before glaring at her. "I'm wearing a fucking *suit*!"

She points those speartipped brown eyes at my pants, not even flinching at the bulge, like she either didn't notice or doesn't care. "That's not a suit. That's the reason those stores that have going-out-of-business sales are going out of business." She sighs, crosses her arms beneath her boobs, and taps her foot. "But seriously. Where's the Principal? I don't have time for this shit."

"Neither do I," I snap, my green eyes narrowed like a viper's as I try not to imagine pushing my forked tongue past those sunset lips just to shut her up. "I *am* the Principal, and you don't have an appointment."

"I don't need an appointment. What happened to Sally? I liked Sally."

"Sometimes shit happens that you don't like," I say, my unblinking gaze trained on those eyes. "Now, if you'll excuse me, I have work to do, like it or not." I step up to her, assuming she'll back up like most people do when they see a towering block of bearded muscle advance on them. But she doesn't even blink, and I'm forced to stop before I run into her curves—which would not be good on multiple fronts (not least of which is the Colonel in my pants that's calling for a full-frontal offensive . . .).

"What's your name?" she says, looking me up and down again, this time blinking just as her gaze sweeps past my blitzkrieg of a boner.

"What's yours?" I counter.

She takes a breath. "Remy. Your turn."

"Principal Rhodes," I say.

She rolls her eyes. "Gimme a break. First name, please."

I grunt and look down my nose at her. She's arrogant in a way that rivals my own obnoxious ass, and although that's usually a big turn-off for me, for some reason my cock is acting like this is the second coming of the goddess herself. It's throwing me off balance, making my head spin as my cock throbs. I've always had a thing for submissive women who'll call me Sir and bend over for their daily lesson, but I don't think Ms. Remy has ever called a man Sir.

I don't back down, and I stay silent, left eyebrow raised, my thick arms folded over my chest as I fight back the fantasy of putting her over my knee, pushing up that brown skirt, yanking down her panties, and having the flat of my hand show her who's in charge.

She shrugs and pulls out her phone. Two finger-taps later she snorts and puts it away. "Rick Rhodes," she says. Then a pointed glance like she's testing me. "I'll call you Ricky."

My head almost explodes as a curtain of red rage comes down behind my eyes. My neck thickens and tightens as I fight back a roar, and it's only when the screech of blood in my temples subsides do I see how much she's enjoying this.

"Ricky," she whispers, those brown eyes taunting me in a way that tells me she'd love to be in a secret prison interrogating some asshole terrorist. She'd get off on it. Twist the knife just because she can. "You hate that, don't you?"

"There's plenty of things I hate," I growl, the daggers of my green gaze meeting the spearheads of her brown eyes. "That's one of them. Never call me that again."

"I'll call you what I want," she says without blinking. "Now, are you going to fire that teacher who yelled at my son or do I need to go above your head and get the School Board involved?"

I glance up at the ceiling, which looks like it's only two feet above my thick head. What's with these low ceilings and tiny-ass desks? I feel like Gulliver in the miniature land of Lilliput—which is a bad sign, because I don't think that story ended well for old' Gulliver.

"You're Fry's mother," I say softly, closing my eyes and just managing to hold back an f-bomb. "Look, he called one of my teachers an idiot, and he was reprimanded for it. I've got my teacher's back on this. Your son needs to learn how to treat people with respect."

I see a shadow pass across her face like dark clouds moving over the land. But before the thunder comes, I shake my head, circle around her, place my hand carefully at the small of her back, and gently push her out of my office. Then I close the door in her face, smiling inwardly when I see her lips part, eyes go wide, color streaking across her cheeks like she's never *not* had the last word.

"Nobody gets the last word with me," I mutter as I lock the door and strut back to my desk, grinning when I hear her rattle the knob and then rap on the frosted glass pane. "Nobody."

2
REMY

"*Nobody* shuts a door in my face," I shout, slamming my hands on the steering wheel as I screech my red BMW SUV out of the school driveway where I'd parked in a handicap spot just because school security knows my car and knows what would happen if they dared tow it.

I glare at my phone as I pull onto the highway, and curse when I see I'm already late. I decide to blame Rick Rhodes, and my cheeks get hotter until I feel beads of angry perspiration on my brow. I'd come close to taking off my heels and smashing in the frosted glass on the asshole's door—and I might have actually done it if I weren't running late.

"I'm on my way. Don't commit to anything until I get there," I bark into the phone after dialing the office. I can almost hear the eye-roll through the phone, but my employees know better than to argue they can handle things without me. I don't trust them to handle a paint-by-numbers game, let alone a million-dollar deal.

I make it to the office and storm into the conference room like I'm trying to stop a murder. To my surprise my team's got the presentation up on the screen and our client is smiling and nodding his bald head. I stay silent as every head turns, and then I quietly take a seat against the wall, nodding at my team leader to continue.

She's as surprised as I am—after all, I don't give up control easily. Or ever. I don't know if I'm still fuming from getting a door slammed in my face or if it's something else about Principal Rick Rhodes that's got me turned around, but I'm most certainly spinning—both my mind and my body.

The presentation's going well, and I allow myself to relax. I'm cooler now, and finally I concede that despite his arrogance, there was something about Rick Rhodes that got to me. Got to me in *that* way. The way a man gets to a woman.

I watch my team leader glow as she answers the

client's questions with a poise that makes me wonder why I don't let her run with things a bit more.
And when I see the client shake hands and then
sign on the dotted line, I rub my chin and nod ap-
provingly at the team.

I mumble out a congratulations before hurrying
out of the conference room. My throat feels thick
like something's stuck inside, and it's only when I
get to my office and slam the door that I realize it's
a ball of emotion. Like something's bubbling up in
me. Something without a name.

"Ohmygod, you are *not* having a nervous break-
down," I say out loud, slumping into my chair and
stroking my neck like I'm calming down a pet. I
know I push myself harder than anyone else in the
office so I can set an example from the top down.
And of course I push myself equally hard at home,
since it's just me and Fry and a dog named Dog. I
don't know why I ever relented to Fry's *Please-can-
we-get-a-dog* chants from age five through seven. I
knew I'd have to take care of the critter. Bath-day
is the worst. Dog's a Retriever and Collie mix, and
there's *so* much hair!

I brush my hair with the purple ceramic brush
I keep in my desk. Long, deep breaths like they
showed me in yoga class before I called the instruc-

tor a good-for-nothing hippie and stormed out after she tried to get me to twist my big body into a pretzel. But the breathing seems to be working, and I feel the tension melt away as the stiff bristles massage my scalp. It feels so good I almost smile, but smiling doesn't come easily to me, especially when I know that a moment of peace only means there's a crisis around the corner.

And just as I think it, my black iPhone buzzes. It's Fry's school, and by the time I answer I'm back in that borderline panic zone where adrenaline and caffeine mix like lighter fluid and a match.

"Now what did he do?" I snap.

There's silence on the line, and then a man's voice comes through—deep, languorous, resonant. Its timbre sends warm vibrations down my legs, electric chills up my spine, and gets my head spinning again but in a weirdly exciting way.

"It's Principal Rhodes," he says.

I know it before he says it. "Ricky," I say without thinking. "Oops."

More silence, this time so loud I can hear it. A slow exhale that makes my speakerphone buzz like even my iPhone feels his anger. This Ricky thing really pisses him off, I note. Good to know. I'll save it for when I really need to pull out the big guns and get his arrogant ass fired. Hopefully the Board will get the message and hire someone like Sally. Someone who's sweet and soft and a total push-over, just the way I like.

"Ms. Remy," he says. "We need to talk about your son."

I roll my eyes and sigh. "Heard that before. What did he do now?"

"Nothing new since yesterday. But I've been re-viewing his records, and I'm seeing a pattern. Con-tempt for authority. Highly disruptive in class. Very disrespectful to teachers—particularly male teachers."

"All that sounds pretty healthy," I snap, rubbing my temples and hoping that dull throbbing isn't a migraine rolling in on the slow train. "Thanks for letting me know. I'll talk to him this evening. OK. Bye!"

"Is he in contact with his father?" Rhodes asks like he knows I'm not going to hang up until he says so.

"None of your business."

I hear Rhodes clicking on his computer key-board. "No contact information for the father. Is he deceased?"

I stare at my phone, almost puzzled at his

hard-headedness. Can't he pick up the not-so-subtle cues that I don't want to have this conversation and it's none of his darned business?!

"Yes," I say, swallowing that thickness in my throat before it chokes me. I can't say any more.

"I'm sorry."

"Thanks."

Rhodes clears his throat. "Fry doesn't take the bus," he says.

I frown. "I drive him. Why?"

"Good. So you'll be coming to the school later today. I'll pencil you in for 4 p.m. in my office. Don't be late."

My frown cuts deeper, and that headache is knocking on the door to my skull. "But school's out at 3," I say.

"Fry's got detention," Rhodes says. "And so do you. Don't be late."

And just as I wind up to let loose the wicked winds of winter, he hangs up on me like how he slammed that door on me. Right in my face. Like he always gets the last word. Always calls the shots. Always needs to be in control. I see it in him because it's in me too.

And that's not a good combination, I think as I grip my purple brush so tight my knuckles shine

white. Nope. Two control freaks are *not* a good combination. That shit's a disaster waiting to happen.
Just like lighter fluid and a match.

Of course, even lighter fluid and a match won't
explode without a spark, though.

So that's all I have to do when I see Principal
Rhodes:

Make sure there's no spark.

3
<u>RHODES</u>

Sparks fly off the doorknob from the static electricity crackling off my cheap suit, and I shake it off and pull open the door. It's Remy, and immediately I notice how different her hair looks now that it's dried. I want to touch the thick, languid dark locks, but I remind myself that this meeting is serious, that this is why I'm here, why I spent eight years getting a degree in Education between tours so I'd be prepared to give back in a way I know I can.

"Sit," I say, stepping back and letting her enter. She steps in and stops, her black Michael Kors leather bag pressed against the front of her tailored brown skirt, Gucci sunglasses hanging from the gold-chain strap. She smells of Japanese jasmine with hints of sweet orange and juniper, and I silently sniff the air as she flows past me towards the solitary wooden chair I've placed in front of my pinewood desk.

She grabs the chair that's painted yellow, dragging it forward a few inches.

"No," I say, stepping close to her and dragging the chair back to where I'd placed it. "There. Sit."

She blinks and cocks her head, her red lips parting like she's about to let that sharp tongue have at me. But I look coolly into those eyes, a ripple of delightfully dominant energy flashing through me when I see her flinch deep behind that confident look. Immediately my cock stiffens, and again I wonder what it is about Remy that's got me so hard that I'm questioning my motives for calling her in here.

"One chair in the middle of the room," she mutters, glancing up at the ceiling and then rolling her eyes. "Surprised there isn't a solitary lightbulb hanging down over it. What was your last job? CIA interrogator?"

"Close." I swallow as she takes off her jacket and slings it over the yellow backrest. She's got a black sleeveless mock-turtleneck on that makes her breasts look like the Guns of Navarone aimed straight at my heart. Quickly I turn away before she sees my eyes glaze over, and I stride to my desk and sit down hard.

I stroke my beard and tighten my jaw as I wait for her to stop moving. "You done?"

"Are *you*?" she snaps, flicking her hair back and making my heart do that thing again where it's like I'm in a firefight but with a different kind of target. "What the hell is this about, Rhodes? Do you know I used to be on the School Board? I can make one phone call and have your ass fired."

I shrug. I grunt. I reach out one thick finger and slowly turn the big black desk phone in her direction. No words. I speak better with my eyes sometimes.

She bites her lip and shakes her head like she's counting down from ten. Not sure which way the timer's going though: Is she going to calm down or just explode?

"You done?" I say again, the words coming from that dead calm, rock solid part of myself that's carried me through situations which would make most guys run so fast they'd leave their balls behind.

"Yes," she says, her round cheeks red like apples,

her plump lips almost split from how hard she's biting down. She might not know what I'm doing, but I sure as hell do. I'm breaking her down in small, bite-sized chunks. Making her submit little by little. Moving the chair back to where I'd placed it. Calling every bluff she makes. Getting calmer the closer she gets to the boil.

I know I'm in dangerous territory here. Behind enemy lines where I'm both sides of the battle. I know her son needs help, but I also can't help what I'm feeling for his mother. Asking about Fry's dad was a legitimate question, but I can't deny what I felt when Remy said he wasn't in the picture. Dangerous. Very fucking dangerous. Watch yourself, Rhodes. You can't do much good in the world if you can't channel your own need to control, your own drive to possess, your own desire to dominate. You held that sexual beast in check for eight years in the Army, but now you're a civilian and you're scared of who you'll become without the military's discipline. For some men leaving the military is like being released from prison—you're free of the routine, but then you realize you *need* the routine. It's what controlled the animal in you, channeled your masculine energy into something useful.

And God help you if you don't find a way to channel that energy right when you're a civilian. That's why some ex-military guys go off the rails, lose themselves to drugs or alcohol or crime or worse.

"You know why I took this job?" I say, forcing myself to speak so I don't tumble down the rabbithole of my mind.

She shrugs, sighs, and looks at her phone. Immediately I get up and take the phone from her. Her eyes go bigger than golfballs, but I just toss the phone in my desk drawer and silently sit.

"I used to be like Fry," I say as Remy's head shakes like a bobblehead doll. But she stays quiet, and although maybe she's shellshocked, I sense that it's something else. I can't be sure yet, but I'll know before this meeting is done, before that smiling clock strikes five.

"That's a shame," she says, crossing her arms under her breasts and leaning back in her chair. I see her brown eyes snap into focus, and I know she's back in control of herself. For now, at least. "I hope it doesn't mean he's going to grow up to be like you."

I just about manage to hide my smile. "There's still hope for the kid," I deadpan.

Now she's the one stifling a smile. I wait as she crosses one leg over the other knee and touches her hair. She feels it too, I decide. She doesn't understand it yet, but she feels it.

"How did he die?" I say, holding my gaze steady

when I see her flinch. Rough transition, but I like it that way. Her guard was down after the light-hearted exchange, and I know she won't be able to close up so soon. She'll answer me. She'll give in. She'll submit.

"How does anyone die?" she says softly. "What difference does it make?"

I frown and stroke my beard again. "Fair enough. You don't need to tell me that. Fry knows though, right?"

She narrows her eyes and immediately I know she never told the kid. It's not unusual. Everyone handles something like that in their own way. My mother refused to talk about how my dad died. And back then there was no online searches or fancy crap like that. It was only when I joined the Army at eighteen that I got the story.

"Fry knows what he needs to know," she says. "That his father's dead."

Her pupils dilate just enough to give me pause. I scratch my chin and review what I know about facial expressions and the "tells" of lying.

"You're lying," I blurt out, surprised that I missed it until now. Damn, she's good at controlling her face and eyes and maybe even her body. The way she flicked her hair earlier. The smoothness of how she slung her jacket on the chair. Hell, is she playing her own little game of dominance?! Have I just come face to face with the female version of myself?! How can that possibly end well?!

"Yes. What took you so long to figure it out? I certainly hope you weren't really an interrogator," she says coolly.

I rub my temples and clench my jaw. "So he's not dead. Where is he? MIA? Deadbeat dad? In prison?"

She snorts, her eyebrows dipping in a pissed-off V like she's insulted. She doesn't reply, and I study that face like it's a puzzle. A puzzle I need to solve.

"Let's see . . . " I mutter, leaning back and tapping my lower lip. "Storms into my office without knocking. Calls me a janitor even though I'm in the Principal's office wearing a suit. Threatens to get me fired within ten minutes of meeting me." I close one eye and raise the other eyebrow. "Drives her son to school herself. Lies like a professional. These are all markers of someone who needs to be in control of herself and her environment. In control of the people around her." I pause and lean forward in my chair, focusing my dangerous green gaze dead center between her eyes. "So if I had to guess. I'd say you controlled that part of your life too. The *man* part of your life. That's it, isn't it?

You *chose* Fry's father. Picked him out of a book. Sperm donor. Most likely anonymous. High-end exclusive sperm bank. Health testing on the semen. No surprises. No drama. No man."

Remy exhales slowly all the way through, and when I'm done she's got a lazy smile on that pretty face, her eyes stretched into slits, elbows on the wooden armrest, fingers tented and centered in perfect symmetry.

"You are so done," she whispers. "The sheer arrogance of a man speculating on the most intimate details of my life. And you're the *Principal*? You are so done, Ricky. So fucking done."

A chill goes through me, and I grimace and rub my beard that's starting to get itchy and uncomfortable. I just crossed like a hundred fucking lines with that shit I spouted. I knew I was in trouble the moment she walked in that door. I should have backed off the moment I knew I wanted her. Yeah, I do care about helping every kid in this school, including her son. But now I've compromised myself by letting her get to me. So how do I get out of this? Do I bow my head and admit defeat? Do I apologize and say I crossed a line?

Or do I do what I've always done.

Lean into the wind.

Face the fire.

Seize the day.

And so I exhale long and slow, lean my swivel chair back, raise my heavy legs, and rest my big feet on the table. "Army taught me a lot of things," I say. "One thing I learned early is that when you cross a line in battle, there's no turning back. You just keep going. Play for keeps. So yeah. I crossed a line and got personal with you. But it *feels* personal with you, Remy. I know this feeling. It's gut instinct, the kind of sixth-sense that comes alive on the battlefield. I've had moments where I stopped to tie my boot or fix my pack and a bullet slices through the air where my head was just a second earlier. I feel that sort of buzz in the air when you're around, Remy."

"That a bullet's headed your way? Yeah, that's *exactly* what's happening." Remy's on her feet now. She grabs her jacket, but the silky cloth slides through her fingers and collapses on the floorboards. She curses and bends down, and her sunglasses detach from the purse-chain and clatter to the wood.

She doesn't say another word, but her lips are trembling and her knuckles are white as she storms out of my office.

And I go calm like I'm in the eye of that storm

Because now I know I was right.

"Lucky guess," I mutter, moving my feet on the desk and running my fingers through my hair. But as I stare at my big feet wrapped in wing-tipped Brazilian leather, I can't stop that old memory from popping into my head.

A memory that reminds me why I know so much about screened sperm donors and exclusive sperm banks.

4
<u>REMY</u>

How could he know?

He doesn't know.

Does he know?

He can't know.

Nobody knows.

"Catch him, Mom!" comes Fry's howl as Dog races down the hallway with a pizza-pocket in his mouth, his paws sliding on the smooth oakwood floor as both boy and beast turn the corner and barrel into my study.

"He's part retriever and you'll never get that out of his jaws," I say as Fry and Dog get into a tug-of-war, both of them playfully growling as I smile and shake my head. "Also, you are *not* eating a half-chewed, totally slobbered-on pizza-pocket." I look sternly at Dog, who's rolling his eyeballs up at me as he holds on to his catch in those strong jaws. "And neither are you, for that matter. That stuff's poison to dogs. Let go. Both of you. Now, please."

Both Dog and Fry let go at the same time, and the pizza-pocket drops dead in the middle of my hardwood floor, splattering marinara sauce all over as if to complete the metaphor. I sigh and reach for a box of tissues, pulling Dog away but not before he snags a piece of pepperoni and scurries out like a thief.

Fry watches me clean up, and when I'm done I ruffle his mop of dark hair that's very much from my side of the family. Not those eyes, though, I think as Fry glances up at me with those puppy-dog greens that I know are going to break hearts and melt minds when the time comes.

"You all right?" I say softly. "Didn't get wounded in the Great Battle of the Pizza Pocket?"

Fry shrugs and fidgets like he always does when he's got something to say. I've always encouraged Fry to speak his mind to me. He needs to know that no matter what he's done or what he's said or even what he thinks, my love for him is unconditional. He needs to know that home is a safe place, that even if I get angry it doesn't mean I don't love him.

"What's up?" I say.

Fidgety fingers and a lopsided shrug.

"You upset about detention?"

Fry shows a tiny smile, and those green eyes shine with mischief. "That teacher *was* an idiot," he says. "He said Thomas Jefferson was our Fourth President. But Jefferson was the Third!"

I raise an eyebrow. "You've memorized all the Presidents?"

"What am I, a nerd? I just looked it up on my phone."

I cover my mouth so he doesn't see me smile. I'm supposed to be disciplining him. Still, he's so darned self-confident that I can't help but be charmed by my little guy. Of course, when he grows up that self-confidence could easily manifest as arrogance, but we'll blow that bridge when we come to it.

"Make me one too," I call after Fry as he scampers off to the kitchen for another shot at a pizza-pocket. "Veggie, please."

"Ew, gross!" he calls from down the hall, and I smile again and stroll to the picture window overlooking my rose bushes that are still blooming even though it's early fall.

The swirls of red and pink and white pop against the deep green leaves, and the thorns are long and wicked but as pretty as the petals, in my opinion. They're covered in green velvet, green the color of Fry's eyes.

But not just Fry's eyes, I think as an image of Rick Rhodes drifts past my mind. He has green eyes too.

I catch myself just before my thoughts go down a rabbithole that I've been down before and don't want to visit again. Ever again. There's a reason I went to a sperm bank with the highest standards for their donors and even higher standards when it comes to privacy. I don't want to know the donor. And I sure as hell don't want the donor to know where his seed ended up.

"I know what I need to know," I whisper, placing a fingertip on the cool glass, positioning it in line with a thorn. "That the donor tested off the charts on both health and intelligence markers. That's all I need to know. Anything more would only be a disappointment, just like every real man in my life. I don't want that for Fry. Yes, he's missing out on having a good male role model in his life. But you know what? There aren't that many good male role models around, and Fry's better off with *no* male role model than the current selection of All-American idiots."

I hear the microwave beep, and the smell of piping hot marinara and sizzling peppers floats into the room. I hear Fry's little footsteps approach, and I try to snap myself out of this weird mood. But when I see my son's green eyes sparkling in the sunbeams, my breath catches when I can't help but think of Rick Rhodes and *his* green eyes. It's ridiculous, of course—so ridiculous that even *thinking* it would be preposterous, a clear sign that I've been alone too long and am letting wishful thinking cloud my intelligence.

"Oooh, that looks *so* good," I say to Fry. He nods with a full mouth that's leaking marinara out the sides. Dog's back in the room, and then they're both running to the basement and the big-screen TV. I follow them down the carpeted stairs, taking each step carefully because I've slid down and landed on my big butt more than once on this treacherous descent. Would be nice to have a man around so I could ask him to put a coarse runner carpet on the stairs so I don't risk death every time I want to catch up on *Downton Abbey*.

"Nope," I say when I hear the rat-tat-tat of machine guns crackle through the speakers. "Too violent. How about an animal channel? Consider Dog's viewing preferences too, young man."

Fry groans and pokes the big silver remote three

times and then tosses it on the wicker stool near the overstuffed red couch that thankfully won't show any marinara stains. I nod in approval when the screen fills with the serenity of a herd of wildebeest grazing in the African Serengeti.

"Here it comes, Dog," Fry says excitedly. "Wait for it. Wait for it. Wait for—"

And I turn away in defeat just as a beastly lion leaps onto the screen, going straight for the throat, jaws savage and wide, claws long and wicked like those thorns that protect my roses.

Protection, I think as I leave my two little critters to revel in the violence of the natural world and head up the stairs to the main floor. Protection is the other thing about having a man around. Luckily we don't live in Serengeti. Also, we aren't defenseless cows munching alfalfa while predators watch from the elephant grass, licking their chops and sharpening their claws.

But just then I hear something at the far end of the house, and I freeze up mid-bite, my mouth full as my heart kicks into high gear. I cock my head, my eyes snapping wide open like a deer in the dark. It sounds like something small just hit the side window, down at the far end of the hallway. I listen for a full minute, and then I almost puke when the sound comes again. Is someone tossing pebbles at the window?! Is someone trying to break in?

Silently I slide out of my shoes, tiptoeing to the kitchen and spitting out my food so I don't choke. I put down the plate and then pad over to the knife rack. The meat cleaver is always a good deterrent, I think. But I'm a Chef's-knife kinda cook. It's the most versatile, in my opinion. You can slice, dice, chop, and bone with a good Chef's knife.

My head's humming and my body's buzzing by the time I get to the place where I'll make my stand, and when I see who it is my shoulders slump and I hurriedly hold the knife behind my butt so he doesn't think I'm crazy even though *he* might be.

"Hey, remember me?" says the guy with the missing tooth.

I sigh and nod. "You're the new lawn guy. What was your name again?"

"Duff. I'm Duff."

"Right," I say, snapping my fingers and smiling apologetically. I'm terrible with names. So bad I sometimes just make up names for people and keep calling them that for years. Probably why I don't have a whole lot of friends. "Careful around those rose bushes," I say. "They've got some wicked—ah, you've met the thorns, I see."

Duff holds up a bleeding left thumb, which he proceeds to suck, much to my disgust. "Let me get you a band-aid," I say, trying to meet his gaze before I realize his gray eyes don't track together.

"Aw, thanks," he says, stepping to the open window and draping his arms through, letting them dangle. I hurry to the medicine cabinet, trying not to think of Duff's thumb leaking blood and saliva on my floorboards. Too late, I realize when I see him mesmerized by the blood droplets on the hardwood below the window sill. "Hey, is your husband around?" he says, glancing at my chest as I bend to hand him the band-aid. "I gotta ask him about something."

"You can ask me," I say, crossing my arms carefully over my breasts and taking a single step back.

Duff closes one eye and sticks out his tongue as he applies the band-aid which I can tell isn't going to hold very long. "Nah, it's OK," he says with a wink that might not have been intentional—at least I hope not. "I'll ask him when I see him. When will he be back, you think?"

"Oh, he's here," I say as my throat closes up a bit. "He's working out in the basement. Lifting real heavy today, so I don't want to disturb him."

Duff swallows, his face drooping in a way that's kind of a relief but also not. He nods and mumbles something before tipping his red-and-white hat that's got plastic mesh, a gas-station logo, and maybe three years of sweat and grease stains. He ambles off to the riding mower a few yards away, and I close the window and lock it.

Only later does it occur to me that I never figured out what that sound was, and at the end of the evening, when I tuck Fry into bed and let Dog out for his last call, I do an extra-careful lockdown of all the windows and doors and set the alarm even though I usually don't bother.

And when I finally enter my solitary bedroom all done in white like it's either a honeymoon suite or a funeral parlor, I slide under the covers and turn on my side, glancing at the untouched pillow next to mine, noticing how the mattress slumps down on my side, like something's out of whack, like something's out of balance, like something's missing . . .

Something I never missed before.

Not until I looked into those green eyes that pierced me like thorns.

Green eyes that make me wonder if fate is really a thing, if nature really does have its own intelligence, its own instinct, its own relentless compass that always points true north, always leads a man home . . .

Always leads a man to his own.

5
<u>**RHODES**</u>

"You did that on your own?"

Fry holds the drawing up and I take it from him, doing my best not to stare into those green eyes that feel like a reflection. I know it's just my imagination, just that fucked up fantasy playing over and over—a fantasy I bet every loser who jizzed into a cup for cash gets at some point or another. Of course, for some guys it plays back as a nightmare, with his zombie spawn clawing at him and whispering *Daddy, we're home* as they rip out his heart.

Rein it in, you idiot, I tell myself as I study the strong linework and confident pencil strokes of Fry's sketch. He's only ten, but he's got talent beyond his years. Well, I always sucked at art, I tell myself—not sure if I'm relieved or disappointed. Shit, there I go again with this crazy idea that belongs in a Hallmark movie. If I don't rein it in soon, I'm going to cross a different sort of line with this kid's mother. A line that's beyond ethical, way past moral, well into the straight up wrong.

Not to mention dangerous, I think as I feel her eyes on me from the group of parents gathered near the tents set up for the School Art Fair that raises money for underprivileged kids. Of course, most of the money is raised via the donation table, but the kids get a thrill when someone buys their drawings and paintings and macaroni sculptures or whatever.

"Your mom seen this yet?" I hold the drawing up to the sunlight as Fry shakes his head. "I'll show it to her. Go on. Do another. These will sell like ice-cubes in the desert."

"Won't ice-cubes melt in like two seconds in a desert?" Fry says, scrunching up his face, those eyes sparkling like he's challenging me, totally not intimidated that I'm the Principal—not to mention about forty times his size!

"Yes, but they'll sell out in about half a second, so the math works fine," I say with a wink and a grin. I'm not going to be outdone by a ten-year-old smart-ass. I always get the last word, whether my opponent is man, beast, or boy with green eyes. My green eyes.

"So long as you don't take returns at your ice-cube stand in the desert," Fry shoots back, his gleefully crooked smile lighting me up like a mortar attack at midnight.

I put my hands on my hips and smile coolly like I've got him. "I only accept returns in their original condition."

Fry twists his mouth and tilts his head. "Not bad," he says almost grudgingly. "You're smarter than my teachers. Of course, that isn't saying much. My dog is smarter than most of my teachers."

I choke back my laughter just before it escapes, and quickly I cover my mouth and turn my head so he doesn't see me go red. Finally I compose myself and manage a stern look which doesn't pass muster when I see his green eyes dancing like leprechauns. He's smart as hell and he knows it. Just like when I was his age.

Fuck, I'm doing it again! I wince and shake my head, almost crumpling Fry's drawing as my body tightens and my arms flex. My shirt buttons are strained at the chest, and I wonder if I'm going to pop from holding back something that yearns to come out, to reveal itself, burst into the open!

"What kind of dog do you have?" I manage to say

through a tight smile that would probably scare the shit out of a normal kid.

"Collie-retriever mix."

"Collies *are* pretty smart. What's his name?"

"Dog."

"Dog?"

"Mom named him," says Fry. He turns back to his new drawing, his kid-sized attention span pulling him away from me. "Take it up with her. She hates you, by the way."

I recoil like I've been ambushed by what's a normal jump-cut comment from a distracted kid. I'm tempted to probe deeper, but I'm the Principal and I know I'm being watched by my staff and the parents alike. It's my job to please both groups, which is sometimes hard when so many of the kids are raised like little lords and can be downright rude to their teachers.

So I leave Fry to his masterpiece and do a slow round of the tables, stopping at every group, smiling and gushing at art that's sometimes worse than this thing called "modern" art that I never understood. Art is supposed to show great battle scenes, far as I'm concerned. But what do I know.

"What were saying to my child?" comes Remy's sharp voice from behind me. I sensed her coming and I'm ready for her. I'm at the last table, and I take my time with the earnest little artists, using the moment to gather myself and make sure I don't do or say anything that gets close to the topic that's playing on my mind like a set of dueling pianos.

"He's not just *your* child," are my very first words, and I almost pass out with sheer disbelief. "I mean, Fry's one of my students. This is a school event. They're *all* my children." I hold my thick arms out wide like a crazy dictator, and I know I'm digging myself deeper into this hole that feels like it's got quicksand at the bottom.

Remy's holding a plastic glass of lemonade, her expression frozen like the ice-cubes in her drink. Slowly she brings the glass to her mouth, keeping her eyes on me like a lookout on a hill. I'm frozen too, so much so that I just watch as she absent-mindedly pokes herself in the nostril with the candy-striped straw that she clearly forgot was in her lemonade.

"Straw," I say like an idiot.

"Idiot," she says, frowning at the straw and then firing a look at me.

"Me or you?" I say with a wink.

"Don't wink like that. You look idiotic."

I straighten up as I inhale. "Now I know why Fry's favorite word is idiot. You know that's an extremely offensive word in today's world."

"Do I look like I give a fuck?" she snaps, trying the straw once again and nailing it this time.

I glance around at the kids as my blood rises. This woman really gets to me, and she darned well knows it. For a moment I entertain the pleasant fantasy of putting her over my knee and spanking her bottom in front of the school and all the parents. But though that might have been fine in the 1700s, it's probably a bit extreme for an Art Fair with ten year olds.

One of whom is mine.

I groan inwardly and rub my beard so hard I give myself rug-burn. I'm losing my mind to some crazy delusion that would be far-fetched even in a dream. Hell, that sperm bank wasn't even in this city! Not even *close*! Besides, even if Fry *is* my son (which he's not), I have no right to call him my son. Talk about walking a dangerous line. Man, this makes those firefights in the desert feel like playtime in the sandlot!

"Look, Remy," I say, standing as close as I dare. Too close, I think when I smell her sweet scent swirling through the freshness of her lemonade.

"No, *you* look," she snarls, poking me in the chest with her right index finger. "What you said the other day was inexcusable. The only reason I haven't complained to the Board is because I've been too busy with work. But I'll get to it, trust me. Now stay the hell away from my son."

"He likes me," I say.

"He does *not*."

"Says I'm smarter than most of the teachers. Almost as smart as his dog—which is high praise." I close my left eye and flash a lopsided grin. "You named your dog . . . Dog? Really?"

"*You're* the dog," she mutters, sucking on that candy-striped straw and looking up at me with big brown eyes that are most definitely *not* in puppy-dog mode.

"Keep 'em coming," I snap. "It just tells me I was right about you."

"You don't know a *thing* about me."

"I know one thing."

"You know nothing."

I take a breath to calm down. Although I've learned to control my temper, I can be a hothead when someone's in my face like this. I'm always the last man standing after a fight—doesn't matter if it's words or bullets. I'm hyper-aware that people are looking at us, but I'll be damned if I'm turning away from something that's activating my soldier's sixth sense like never before. I felt it the moment

Remy walked into my office. I felt it when I looked into Fry's green eyes. And I feel it now.

Remy sucks down the last of her lemonade, but she's still here. I frown, my breath catching when I see her looking into my eyes—well, not quite: More like she's looking *at* my eyes.

And now it hits me that shit, Remy noticed the same thing I did, didn't she? Fry's green eyes. I bet no one in her family has green eyes, so she must know Fry got that from his anonymous father. Is that why she's attacking me but can't pull away? Does she hate the idea that fate might have brought us together, screwed up her perfect little plan about life without a man?

I'm about to just put it out there, straight up tell her where and when I donated my swimmers. Maybe we can talk about this like adults instead of taking shots at each other while dancing around what's really got us all turned around. Hell, maybe she'll even say let's do a DNA test!

My heart jumps up to my throat, fear and excitement spiraling up my neck and down my spine as I get that strange feeling like I'm in a dream. I used to get that otherworldly sense out in the desert, where you catch a glimpse through the veil of reality, see the universe winking at you from the shadows, reminding you that it's all a trick, all a joke, all a game that's been played through eternity, through every cycle of life and death. That sense of play is what's kept me alive through the bloodiest of battles—the inexplicable certainty that a man's got a destiny to fulfill, and so long as he stays true to his heart, true to his duty, true to his personal moral code, no bullet will ever find its mark before he finds his fate.

And I've found my fate, I decide as I gaze upon Remy's face, see the unspoken truth behind those brown eyes, feel her intuition speaking through her short, anxious breaths, like she's got that same feeling of being about to pop if she doesn't speak her mind, face that unspoken question, face the chance that—

"Oh, shit, what are the chances?" comes the interruption just as I'm open to blurt out something I can't take back. My mouth's already open, and I slowly close it and take a rumbling breath as I recognize the voice.

It's Duff, and from his dark green overalls and white sewed-on nametag I see he's working for the contracting service we use for groundskeeping in the school. One look into his bloodshot eyes and I see he's not quite right. Maybe not sleeping. Maybe something else.

But Duff's grinning at Remy, and I stiffen when

he holds up his right thumb that's swollen like an infected apple. "Thorn? Band-aid? Remember? Shit, you don't remember me?"

Remy blinks and offers a tight smile. "Oh, yes. The new lawn guy," she says, wincing and trying not to get too close to his thumb. "You work here at the school too?"

"Yeah, they send me all over town," Duff says, turning to me with a wassup nod that I don't return. "Hey, Rick. Nice suit, man! Hey, listen, I gotta talk to you about that thing from last week." He tugs at his nametag. "Maybe we can do something about getting my wife's kid in—seeing that I'm an employee and all now."

I smile stiffly and exhale slow. "You're a subcontractor, not an employee. She's your ex-wife, not your wife. And that isn't even your kid."

My annoyance rises as Remy raises her eyebrows and then backs away. Duff's too close for comfort, and I sidestep him before he starts up again.

"La Jolla, California," I say to Remy just before she turns away.

"What?" she says, her head jerking towards me like an invisible puppet-master is in control.

I stay silent for a long moment, that surreal calmness washing over me when I see the lights almost go out for her. Not for me, though. For me the lights go on like it's football night at WestPoint.

Yeah, the lights are shining bright, and they're shining on me, on my fate, on my future, on my . . . family.

A family that I'm going to claim.

Both the child and the woman.

My child.

And my fucking woman.

6
<u>REMY</u>

I inhale another sugary lemonade just to keep the lights on in my short-circuiting head.

La Jolla, California.

There's no way he could have known that if he hadn't . . . if he didn't . . . if he wasn't . . . if he isn't . . .

"No," I say out loud, smiling with my sticky lips as I walk to the back of the tent and stare out over the lush green lawn towards the smooth brown dirt of the baseball diamond down the way. The white bleachers are shining in the sun, and I squint as the flashes make me dizzy. "There's no way. That's just impossible. Too unbelievable. Real life doesn't work that way. Shit, even *made-up* life doesn't work that way! I don't even think a romance writer would try a plot this ridiculous!"

I turn my body halfway and glance sideways at Rhodes, who's still talking to that creepy groundskeeper with the zombie thumb. Rhodes towers over the man, his shoulders twice as broad, hair stiff and thick like a battle-king's head-dress. For a moment I think of what I said about my imaginary husband working out in the basement, pumping iron so he can be big and strong to protect his family. *I am man! Hear me roar!*

I try to roll my eyes but I can't do it. Hearing those words flipped a switch in me, and I almost double over as the butterflies go nuts in my tummy. I'm scared out of my mind, but not in a fearful way. It's like being scared before doing a big deal at work—I know I want this deal, but I also know it won't be easy, that making the deal brings a crapload of complications with it.

Rhodes finally gets rid of Duff, and he glances over at me before I can look away. Those green eyes look even more familiar from afar, and I touch my neck and make myself turn away before I *can't* turn away.

I sense him moving towards me, but when I glance over my shoulder I see one of the other moms stop him to introduce herself and sweet-talk him for her kid's sake. I sigh and glance at my phone before turning my attention to where Fry's waving to me and holding up a drawing.

I smile warmly and maneuver my wide hips between the tables to make my way over to my son. Again I can sense Rhodes turn his attention to me, to Fry, to . . . to us. I can't explain it, but I feel it as clearly as I feel the sun on my neck. There's something happening here, and if I didn't know better I'd say it was fate, destiny, meant to be.

But of course I *do* know better. Fate is what you create. Destiny is what you design. As for meant to be? Well, that's just an excuse for when you lose control of your life.

"Aw, is that you and me?" I say to Fry, blinking away what feels like tears even though it can't be tears because I don't cry, never cry, can't cry, *won't* cry. I take the drawing from Fry's little fingers, sighing when I see a pretty good rendition of my red BMW with two people in the front.

"No," says Fry.

I frown and take a closer look. Now I notice that although it's clearly me behind the wheel, the figure in the passenger seat isn't a child. It's a man. A man with stiff black hair like a battle-king's mohawk. A man with a thick beard that could give a bear rug-burn. A man in a brown suit. A man with green eyes that leap off the page and right into my heart, into that place where nothing makes sense and everything makes sense.

I ruffle Fry's hair and take his hand gently, leading him out of the tent without saying a word. I can't be here, not with Rhodes standing there, calmly talking to parents and teachers even though I sense his attention on me and Fry like we're all connected, like we're his family, like we're just straight-up *his*!

By the time we drive out of the lot I'm somewhat calm, almost back in control of my life and myself. We take a left on Maple Street and I tap the brakes and glide to a soft stop at the crosswalk for a young couple with a baby carriage and a puppy. The woman smiles at us for stopping, and I smile back. Her eyes are bloodshot but happy, her cheeks droopy but glowing, her gait slow but springy. I glance at Fry, taken by how intently he's watching the family.

We ride in silence the rest of the way, like we're both lost in our own worlds. I pull into the driveway and park at an awkward angle, the front left wheel on the grass. We hear Dog howling out his welcome from inside, and I sigh and relax as I look forward to my feet landing on solid, familiar ground.

But then Fry glances over at me, drops his gaze down to his rolled-up drawing sticking out of my bag, and then locks those green eyes with mine.

"Is Principal Rhodes going to be my Dad?" he asks.

I stare like he's an alien speaking in tongues. My throat closes so hard I have to tap my neck so I can breathe again. I don't know where that came from, but I can sure as hell guess.

"What did Principal Rhodes say to you?" I ask, my jaw tightening when I remember the two of them talking at the Art Fair. If Rhodes *dared* to say *anything* about—

But I stop when I see the passenger seat is empty and both the car door and the back door are open. Dog is frenzied happy like he hasn't seen a human in days, and Fry's tearing across the lawn like he's some kind of animal himself. So I just sigh and sink back behind the wheel and let them play their game.

"Maybe it's *all* a game," I mutter, rubbing my aching temples and dabbing the corners of my moist eyes with my cold white knuckles. I put down the window and rest my elbow on the door, letting my thoughts drift along with the lazy breeze. My gaze lands on those rose bushes near the side wall, and then I absentmindedly think of that guy Duff and his big red thumb.

Now I feel the Rhodes tension creep through me again, and my breathing quickens as my mind tries to seize control once again. Before I can stop myself I'm spinning through the possibilities—the *realistic* possibilities.

And random chance is *not* realistic. If Rhodes really is Fry's biological father, there's no way all three of us could have just *happened* to meet in this town, this school, this moment in time. We're hundreds of miles from California. If it's just coincidence, then everything I believed about the world is wrong. We might as well be living in an enchanted forest with unicorns prancing about, stabbing their uni-horns through magical strawberries that giggle when you eat them.

The tension oozes through me, tightening my muscles, twisting my sinews, tickling my throat until I'm wound up and tied down all at once. And through it all comes the cold, calculating truth— or what *has* to be the truth: That Rhodes used his military connections to figure out if his donated sperm ever made it out into the world.

And immediately there's an overwhelming rush of relief, like I'm back in control, back in the world of cause-and-effect, where luck and randomness don't exist outside of a casino. In my world, if something's too crazy to be true, it probably *isn't* true.

"Well, that's that," I say firmly as I push open the door and slide my butt off the smooth leather seat. I grab my things and look for Fry. He's nowhere to be seen, but I hear him messing with Dog near the old swing set that's still there even though Fry doesn't play on it and I'd already decided I was never having another child. That was the plan. One and done. No man. No marriage.

And no chance of a mistake.

Except the one that maybe I'm about to make now, I think as I head to my study and close the door and turn on my oversized iMac Pro. My fingers fly across the silver keyboard, and I slump in the leather swivel chair and read the words on the screen:

DNA Testing, it reads, and a sickening sensation creeps through me as I hear Fry slam the back door and yank open the fridge. Something about it makes me want to throw up, like I don't know if what I'm considering is right or wrong, if I want to know or not, if my son should know or not!

"But what's my other option?" I whisper. "Have my son attend Rhodes' school for another eight years with the question hanging out there, casting its shadow over me and Rhodes and probably Fry too?

And shit, Fry's *already* sensing something's up with Principal Rhodes, isn't he? What was that question about Rhodes becoming his Dad? Fry's *never* asked that about a man before! Sure, I haven't been dating for years now, but even when I was dating a little Fry never asked those innocent, unfiltered questions.

Now I take a sharp breath and lean forward and slap the power switch on my computer. The screen goes black, and I feel like it matches something inside of me. A part of me I don't understand. A part of me I don't *want* to understand.

It's a part of me that . . . that *wants* it to be true.

Ohmygod, I *want* it to be true!

And now I break down like a car in the rain, the tears that threatened all the way home coming hard and quick, big drops rolling down my cheeks as I sob noisily, my shuddering body making the chair squeak on its springs. The sobs come from places so deep it's like I'm digging into dangerous parts of my psyche that were buried like unexploded bombs, waiting for just the right moment to explode and shatter the calm earth that hid them so long.

7
RHODES

"It's an unexploded bomb that just sits there under the soil, waiting for someone to disturb its peace so it can fulfill its destiny. And what is a bomb's destiny if not to fucking explode and destroy everything in sight?"

I stare at my laptop screen that's shining with the staid off-white background that says *DNA Testing* in unadorned blue letters. I'm sick to my gut from where my mind's been dragging me these past few hours. I haven't eaten. Haven't changed my clothes. Haven't worked out. All I'm thinking about is Remy and Fry, my soul clenching inside me like a fist, my body twisting like a tornado, both parts of me threatening to tear me apart one moment, crush me to dust the next.

For one dark moment I'd considered getting Fry's DNA off a cup or fork in the cafeteria and running the tests without telling Remy. But the thought made me so sick I doubled over and retched. I'm not that guy. No way I can do that—no matter what the result.

"So who are you then?" I ask myself out loud, finally ripping off my tie and collapsing into the rough leather couch that's been with me since La Jolla. I think back to the man I was back in California. It was after my second tour, and one of my buddies had just had his sperm frozen and stored just in case something happened to him before he married his fiancée and knocked her up.

"That way she'll have the option of still having my kid, you know?" he'd explained when we caught up for a drink near the base in San Diego. "You should think about it, Rick. That shit's important. Every life form has the instinct to reproduce. Even a blind-ass worm will find a way to wriggle its way to a mate just to pass on its genes. You can fight anything out there, Rick. But this ain't out there. It's in here," he said, tapping the center of his chest, right above his heart. "Can't fight what's in here, man." Then he'd sipped his Michelob Golden and grinned. "Well, I guess you can fight it. But you ain't gonna beat it. It'll get you in the end, one way or another."

I'd laughed it off at the time. I was a freewheeling stud back then, and the last fucking thing I wanted was a kid. Fatherhood was *not* in my gameplan, and I laughed off that whole freezing-my-boys thing.

But the seed was planted, and I guess those words stuck with me, because later that summer, when I signed up for my third Tour, I felt a little something inside me. A little voice that whispered the ancient truth that even the blind worm knows. And the truth always comes out, one way or the other.

Of course, my freewheeling, gunslinging self at the time still didn't want anyone calling me Daddy (except in *that* way, if you know what I mean . . .), and so when a friend in the healthcare world told me about this private, high-end place in La Jolla that would pay three grand for one "discharge" if I passed their tests or whatever, I said what the hell. Just like a tree sends it seeds out and lets the wind and rain carry them wherever, I'll leave it up to chance, let fate have at it, bid destiny goodluck and Godspeed.

I just didn't know destiny was a boomerang.

And it's got me dead in its sights.

So what do I do? Try to duck? Try to run? Try to hide?

Nah.

That ain't my jam.

I lead the charge into battle.

Face the onslaught like a soldier.

Leave it all on the field.

And the moment I make the decision to follow my instinct, chase my intuition, trust my heart, something opens up in me, revealing another truth, a truth that I'd known and forgotten.

The truth that my heart didn't lead to my son. After all, I'd seen Fry the week before when he got hauled to my office for calling that teacher names. And it's not like I looked into his mischievous green eyes and somehow "knew" he was my kid. No. That's not what got my heart beating, my blood pumping, my mind focused. Nah, it wasn't the child.

It was the woman.

And with a whooping war cry I'm off the couch and out the door, furiously tapping my phone so I can get Remy's address from the encrypted school directory. Two minutes later I'm burning rubber down Main Street, my heart thumping out a victo-ry-beat, my soul singing this solider home.

8
<u>REMY</u>

"Nobody home. Go away," I mutter when the door-
bell sounds for the second time in three seconds.
If I were alone I'd sit quiet and wait for whoever it
is to give up and leave. But of course Dog's barking his head off and I already hear Fry's bare feet
thumping on the hardwood as the two of them race
each to the front door.

"Hey, kid," comes a man's voice as I round the
corner. The sun just set and the hallway is gloomy
like a storm's coming. "Your Dad home? I gotta ask
him about something?"

I hurry to the door, my throat tightening as I try
not to run. It's that guy Duff, and he's still in the

green overalls that look significantly filthier than when I saw him this afternoon at the school. He's got a pair of large hedge-trimmers dangling from his left hand like a rusty claw, and I try not to panic when I see how his gray eyes move like pinballs in a broken machine.

Somehow I get to Fry before Duff gets a response that will make it clear there's no man in the house. "Take Dog to the other room, OK?" I say softly to Fry. Then I pull my cotton button-up tight over my breasts and smile. "He'll be home any minute," I say calmly. "Just getting done at the shooting range, and he likes to clean his guns before bringing them home."

Duff closes one pinball eye and squeaks the hedge-trimmer like it helps him think. Then he nods and rubs the back of his head, tipping his hat forward accidently. He grins and pulls the hat back, looking past me into the house as I debate whether slamming the door right now would be rude. I have no problem being rude, but this guy unnerves me. I almost feel sorry for him, but I also sense an edginess that makes me wary.

Again I get that sickening feeling that it would be nice to have a man around. I don't like thinking that way. I've never thought that way before.

I'm not some helpless housewife who screams and faints when she sees a bee in the kitchen. Then again, I've never felt threatened in my own home before. Why is this happening now? Why is *any* of this happening now?!

"Now's not a good time, OK, Duff?" I say sweetly as I back away so I can close the door. "And listen, there's no need to stop by for the next couple of weeks. I'll call the contractor and let them know."

Duff's sunburned cheeks droop like leather saddle-bags. "So . . . like . . . I should come back next week?"

"I'll call the contractor and work it out," I say, stretching the smile until I feel the strain beneath my ears. "Thank you for—"

"Hey, are you *firing* me?!" Duff snaps, jamming his palm against the door, those hedge-trimmers squealing like a distant bird of prey. "Listen, Lady, they don't pay me if I don't have any work. I need this money. I got alimony payments and back taxes and medical bills and I'm behind on the rent."

Duff's laundry list of problems sounds like the agenda for a daytime talk show, and I try not to patronize him with my smile. "Oh, there's my husband now!" I say suddenly, glancing past him and smiling like someone's there. Duff takes his hand off the door so he can turn, and I seize the moment to swing the door as hard as I can.

But Duff's twitchy eyes catch my movement, and just before the latch clicks shut he slides those hedge-trimmers between the door and the frame! Then he *rams* his shoulder into the door, sending me stumbling back. I yelp as I feel the runner rug move under me, and I grab the side-table to keep from falling.

Of course, the table is tall and slender like a sapling, and it tips over and sends a blue-and-yellow Tiffany lamp to the hardwood. The lampshade shatters and now Dog starts up from the other room, a hollow, bloodthirsty bark that I know means business.

"You keep that dog locked up!" Duff screams, stomping into my home with those hedge-trimmers swinging, his free hand reaching for my throat and gripping tight.

"Fry, stay there with Dog!" I shout, hoping to hell that Fry listens for once. I also hope he's got his phone with him and is already dialing 911. I twist my neck away from his grip, and then I swing my fists wildly even though it's been ten years since I took that self-defense class.

He steps back and I punch empty air, and when

I try again I scream when my fingers collide with that hedge-trimmer! I'm not hurt bad, but it sounds bad enough to Fry, and I hear him burst into the hallway to protect his mother.

"You stay away from my Mom!" Fry screams as he rushes into the fight. Dog's loose now too, and I scream when I realize both Fry and Dog could get badly hurt!

I brace myself to defend my son and dog as they rush out to defend me. Duff looks taller and more ominous in the shadowy hallway, and he's got that hedge-trimmer snapping like a sea-turtle. Dog's standing beside me, barking like a rabid beast as Duff howls and swipes wildly at us with the rusty blades.

And then another shadow falls over the scene.

It's coming from the open front door, and I gasp when I see that it's Rhodes in the doorway, his broad frame blocking almost all the light, casting him in silhouette, wide and tall like a protective superhero with a cape and wings.

In one smooth motion Rhodes grabs Duff by the shoulder and spins him around, cracking him on the jaw with a perfect punch that's timed with the spin. Those hedge-trimmers fall just as Duff drops, and Rhodes chooses to catch the trimmers so they don't scuff my floorboards.

Duff hits the floor like a bag of rice, and Rhodes glances down to make sure the guy is out cold. He is.

"Woo hoo!" Fry howls, raising both hands and prancing about the hallway in his bare feet. Dog is almost frothing at the mouth from the frenzy, but although he's still barking, it's the good kind of bark. The bark that says all's right in the world, all's good in the land. all are safe in the family . . .

Because Daddy's home.

9
<u>RHODES</u>

I finish up with the police and wait out on the curb for the last car to leave. Then I turn back to the house, stopping and smiling when I see Remy and Fry and Dog on the front stoop. Remy's got her arm draped over her son, and Dog's got his pink tongue flopping about like he's grinning at me.

I take my time walking up the pebbled path, trying to shake off the weird feeling like this is my family, my home, my . . . my *life*! But it's not, even though it felt like it after that short-lived fight when both Remy and Fry hugged me at the same time and I kissed each of them on the cheek like they were mine to kiss.

"There'll be assault charges," I say quietly once Fry takes Dog out to the back so both of them can release some of that nervous energy. "Duff's already rattled off a long statement that will probably be enough to make the charges stick. He'll get a public defender who'll make a deal. Some jail time and hopefully some counseling to help get his head right."

"Good." Remy nods as we stand by each other. The sun is gone, but the horizon is streaked with deep purple and dark indigo, slim clouds dressing the corners of the scene as Venus watches us from her solitary perch. "Come inside," she says softly.

I shove my hands into my trouser pockets. I'm still wearing the brown suit from this afternoon, though I left the tie and jacket on my couch. Remy touches my arm lightly. Then she squeezes my forearm, and when I look into her brown eyes I'm reminded of why I came here. Yeah, it's tempting to think I was mysteriously drawn here by the magical universe so I could protect my son, my flesh-and-blood. But I know that I'm here for Remy first. I'm here by choice, not by coincidence. I'm here for her.

"Listen," I say. "What I said this afternoon about La Jolla . . . it was . . . it crossed a line. Can we start over?"

Remy looks up at me, her hand still gripping my forearm, her fingers soft and warm against my hard muscle. "What's wrong with where we are now?"

"Where *are* we now?"

Remy shrugs and bites her lip. "I don't know. Come inside."

I glance at the heavy oak front door with its gold brass knocker. I look up at the red brick facade, the green wood window frames, the rose bushes overflowing with red and pink and yellow blooms that shine under the starlight of Venus. I look down into Remy's brown eyes again, feel her hand on my arm, smell her scent that's sweeter than the roses. Does she know I'm here for her and her alone? Does she know that even though I've been led here by fate, *she's* my fate, not anything else, not anyone else? Does she know that it doesn't matter if Fry is my biological son or not?

It doesn't matter.

It never mattered.

My heart wasn't pulling me to him.

It was pulling me to her.

10
<u>REMY</u>

I pull the red kettle off the gas burner and fill our yellow ceramic cups. Rhodes straightens his back and dips both tea bags at once, his thick arms moving in tandem with military precision. He's sitting at the granite-topped kitchen island that's never had a man lean his big elbows on it. Not a real man, at least.

I roll my eyes and shake my head as I turn away and place the kettle on an oven-mitt. It's hard to believe how much my inner world has changed since Rick Rhodes parachuted into my life, launching a full frontal assault—or maybe an ambush. All I know is that I'm suddenly having thoughts I didn't have even when I was pregnant with Fry. Back then I was younger and so self-confident it bordered on arrogance. I could do anything on my own. More importantly, I *wanted* to do everything on my own.

And *that's* what changed, I decide as I dry my hands and pad barefoot across the kitchen tiles to the island where Rhodes is keeping watch. I still *can* do everything on my own. But I no longer want to. I want something different. Something more. Something that's always been missing.

"Fry isn't missing anything not having a Dad. I never knew my old man, and I turned out fine," Rhodes says as I slide my butt onto the wicker-topped stool and cross one leg over the other knee. My skirt hikes up my thigh, and Rhodes takes a sharp breath though his eyes don't move down.

I feel things tighten under my skirt, and I clear my throat and sip my jasmine tea, hoping it'll clear my head. I hear Fry and Dog playing Frisbee in the well-lit backyard, and after another warm sip my neck muscles finally soften, my shoulders relaxing as I allow myself to just be in this moment.

"Is that why you never had kids?" I say before biting my lip and going flush when I realize how that statement just *might* be false.

Rhodes holds up his teacup to hide his grin. I smile and look down at the speckled granite between us. "I didn't come here to talk about kids," he says, dabbing his lips with a paper napkin that's got balloons and birthday cake on it. He frowns at the napkin and then those green eyes go serious. "I came here to talk about us, Remy."

I touch the side of my neck. My hand is still warm from the teacup. "So talk," I say, crossing my feet at the ankles. My toes feel tingly, and I wiggle them and smile. I feel so young, it suddenly occurs to me. Like we're two teenagers about to have the *I-like-you-do-you-like-me* conversation in her parents' kitchen. Somewhere in my mind that grown-up woman reminds me that I'd decided Rhodes had used his military connections to find me and track me and now he's using his charm to . . . to what? Steal my son?

For some reason that sounds ridiculous and paranoid even though earlier today it seemed like the most logical explanation. But now, with Rhodes sitting at my kitchen island like he belongs here, with those green eyes seeming more familiar by the second, with his masculine scent infusing my senses like smoky tea-leaves . . . now everything just flipped to its opposite. Now it feels like maybe that craziness about fate and destiny is the most logical explanation. After all, what are the chances we all ended up at the same school? What are the chances that both of us felt sparks the moment we were in the same room? What are the chances Rhodes showed up just when Fry and I were threatened?

He could have sent Duff over to threaten you so he could swoop in just in the nick of time like some hero, whispers that smart, no-nonsense business-woman who's always in control. You saw Rhodes talk to Duff at the Art Fair. This is a setup.

It *is* a setup, I respond to that woman as Rhodes stays quiet because Fry just burst into the house to grab some dog treats. Boy and animal are gone in a flash, and I'm left pondering something that makes my body tingle, makes my heart thrum, makes my soul soar:

It is a setup, I decide through that tingle.

But we've *both* been set up.

Set up by the universe.

Set up by fate.

Rhodes puts his cup down and stands. He's right by me now, facing me as I try not to look up into his eyes. He hasn't said a word after the interrup-tion. He's not going to say a word. And you know what? I don't need him to say a darned word. I know he came here for me, that all of this started with me and him ten years ago . . . ten years before we ever met.

He brushes my cheek with the back of his rough

hand, gazing into my eyes and then gently sweeping a strand of hair from my forehead. My nose tickles and I wrinkle it up like that girl in her mama's kitchen. Now there's that feeling again, that deep, yearning feeling that I thought I'd never seek, that desperate longing to give up control, for just a moment, to someone I trust . . . trust with my child, trust with my life, trust with my love.

"I want to say something but I won't. Not yet," Rhodes whispers, his breath warm against my cheeks. I move my ass on the stool. My left knee brushes the front of his trousers, and a wave of heat travels up my skirt when I feel him harden.

"Way to keep the suspense going," I whisper back through a smile, my fingers curling along with my toes as Rhodes draws his lips dangerously close to mine.

"There's no suspense," he says, his beard tickling my chin and making me shiver in that delightful way like when the fire crackles hot in a chilly room. "No suspense because I already know what comes next."

And before I take the bait and ask the question, Rhodes answers it.

He answers it with a kiss, full on the lips, warm on the mouth.

Right there, in my well-lit kitchen, with the happy calls of child and dog coming through the walls, the sweet smell of jasmine tea in the air, the warm mist of kettle steam clouding the yellow lamplight, he kisses me.

By God, he kisses me.

11

<u>RHODES</u>

The kiss says everything we haven't, everything we can't, everything we won't. It says this is about me and her, and everything else comes later. If this weren't about me and her it would be about nothing.

"Your lips taste better than I imagined," I say, pulling away and smiling as she blushes like a plum.

"You imagined tasting my lips?" She blushes deeper, that bare knee grazing my crotch again, sending me to full mast so quick I almost groan.

"Imagined much more than that." I run my finger down her neck and gently tug at the V of her black top. I kiss her lips again, slide my hand around the back of her neck, kiss her once more, carefully licking the outside of her mouth before drawing back.

She gasps and stiffens, her fingers closing around my wrist as I tighten my grip on her nape. I can see down her top now, and the view of her healthy cleavage tucked into a black bra makes me swoon like a horny kid seeing up a girl's skirt for the first time.

Remy glances at the window, but I shake my head and turn her face back to me.

"Your son is safe," I say firmly. "You're safe. You'll always be safe, Remy."

She blinks twice, looks past me and then into my eyes again. "I shouldn't need you to make me feel safe. I don't *want* to need you to make me feel safe. If I can't make myself and my son feel safe, then I've failed as a mother."

I take a breath and relax my grip, running my hand up her neck, sliding my fingers through her thick tresses. She pushes her head into my palm, smiling and sighing.

"Duff won't be out for a while," I say.

Remy shakes her head and glances up at me. "It's not about him, Rhodes. It's you."

"I make you feel unsafe?"

"No! No." She bites her lip and shakes her head vigorously. "No. It's not you, it's me."

I chuckle. "You already pulling out the old *it's-not-you-it's-me* line? Aw shucks. We didn't even get to the fun parts. We can still do the break-up sex, right?"

Remy giggles as that plum-rose blush comes back. I gently tug on her hair, bringing forth that sigh once more. I feel her shoulders relax, but only for a flash. Now that focus is back in her eyes like she doesn't want to let her guard down.

"Turn," I say. "Face away from me."

She doesn't budge. I don't ask again. I just grab the stool, lift it with her sitting on it, and turn it in the direction I want. Remy starts to protest, but I clamp my hand over her lips and lean in close, my lips almost touching her left ear. "Close your eyes," I say in a warm whisper, my breath making the tendrils of brown hair around her ears move breezily. "Focus on your other senses. Listen to the world around you. Feel the world within you." She mumbles something through my fingers, and I can feel her eye-roll without seeing her face. "You can roll your eyes all you want so long as you keep them closed," I say.

She mumbles again, but I bring my other hand up and press my fingertips between her shoulder blades, grinning as I feel those coiled muscles open up under my stiff touch. I feel the relaxation ripple down her spine, and now I take my hand off her mouth and place both thumbs into the meaty part of her shoulders and push hard.

"Oh, shit, that feels so good," she says, arching her head back, moaning, and then hunching forward. I move my thumbs down her center-line, working each segment of her backbone with tenderness and precision. "Keep doing that."

Immediately I stop, pulling my hands away and crossing my arms over my chest. She arches her head back and pouts up at me, her pretty round face so darned cute all upside-down I almost melt. Almost.

"What happened?" she says.

I shrug and look around like I have no idea what she means.

"Ohmygod, is it because I said *Keep doing that*? You don't like being told what to do?"

I stroke my chin. Then I put one hand behind my back and place the other on her back. "Half right. So you get one hand back. I'm keeping the other for now."

She snorts in disbelief, and I see a flash of annoyance in those eyes. But then I push my thumb against her left scapula, teasing out a knot below the shoulder blade. She groans and exhales, and I smile. Good. She's learning. Learning who I am.

And maybe learning who she is too.

"Half right . . ." she murmurs as I march my fingers down her spine, keeping to the left side only so she feels what's missing, works to get my other hand back on her body. "So I'm not supposed to tell you what to do. Got it. You're the Principal. The hero. The warrior. Note my epic eye-roll. What else am I missing? What's the part I got wrong?"

"Your part."

She wriggles her ass on the stool, trying to maneuver her body so her right side gets my magic fingers. "Stop," I command. "Let go, Remy. Just let go."

Remy exhales hard and jerks her body forward. She reaches behind herself and swats my hand away. I bring my hand back to her spine, tightening my upper arm and shoulder so that when she tries to swat me away again it's like hitting a stone pillar. She tries and fails, and I smile and shake my head. She can slide her ass off the stool and walk away.

She doesn't.

"That's the part I'm missing," she says finally. "To let go. To not try to control every tiny thing in my life. Every person in my life."

I bring my other hand forward and place it on her unattended right side, making her shudder and lean her body into me. "You're learning," I whisper, giving her the two-hand treatment and kissing her neck at the same time.

She moans as I run my lips down her neck, press my fingers into her back, bring my crotch close to her hips from behind. I'm so hard it's obscene, and when she arches her neck back and I see that cleavage calling me close, I slide my hands around and grasp her globes firmly, squeezing hard and making her gasp.

I pinch her nipples and lick her neck, growling when I feel hard points form beneath my rough touch. Her nipples are big and hard, and I want to suck them until she screams. My cock is pressed hard against the top of her ass as she shifts back and forth on the stool, and I feel the man in me rising to where things are going to get very fucking hot. Too hot for this open kitchen.

"Fry could come in at any moment," she says, her eyes firmly closed, tongue snaking in and out as I knead her breasts and lean over her from above. I kiss her cheeks and forehead and finally those lips, my hands moving down along her curves. I squeeze her healthy belly, and then I'm rubbing her thighs,

keeping my other hand firmly on her wet mound, my sticky fingertips teasing her pubic curls as she pants and whimpers. Then I reach both hands beneath her hiked-up skirt, grasp her panties right below her crotch, and tear the cloth at the V. I slide the soaked black satin out from where it had ridden up her asscrack, and I put those panties in my trouser pocket just as she slowly flutters her eyelids open. She looks up at me like she'd forgotten where she was, and I smile like that was the entire fucking idea.

"I did that?" she says, glancing at the teethmarks on my middle finger.

I hold it up like I'm flipping her off. She covers her mouth and chokes out a laugh as she straightens her back and jostles her hips to get her skirt down past her ass. Then she notices something missing. She looks at the floor beneath the stool and then glares at me.

"You did *not* just steal my panties."

"I didn't steal them. I earned them." I pat my trouser pocket. "Every soldier plays *Capture the Flag*."

"My underwear is not a flag! Give those back. Now."

I frown and twist the left side of my mouth. "Tell me what to do again and I'll take your bra."

She turns and tries to reach for my trouser pocket. But she stops mid-grab when she sees how peaked I am, how fucking hard and ready I am to stake my claim over every inch of her territory. She casts a wide-eyed look up at me, and then with trembling fingers reaches out and strokes me.

I almost come in my pants, and I have to slam my hand down flat on the granite island to keep myself upright. My vision blurs as she cups my swollen cock and heavy balls and I arch my head back and groan out loud. Still holding on to the table, I slide my hand around the back of her head and pull her close. Remy unzips me and slides her hand inside, somehow getting her fingers through the flap of my boxers. Her touch makes me curse and mutter, and I'm this fucking close to ripping her clothes off, popping her up on the kitchen island, and then fucking her raw under the hot halogen lights of the homestead.

"Mom!" comes Fry's voice from outside the backdoor, and Remy rips her hand away so fast she almost takes my cock with it. I leap back and turn, zipping up as fast as I dare. I take three deep battlefield breaths to slow down my heart and hopefully get my fucking vision to focus again. Then I clear my throat and turn just as Fry and Dog come bounding into the kitchen, both of them hot and flushed.

We're hot and flushed too, but outside we're calm like cucumber sandwiches at teatime. Remy's got her skirt all smoothed out, and her legs are carefully crossed at the knee as I stand beside her, my hand casually placed in front of my telltale bulge.

"We're going upstairs," Fry says, grabbing a box of cereal from the counter and a fresh bag of dog treats from the metal shelf near the dog-bowl. "Dog's gonna watch TV with me. He's sleeping in my room tonight."

"Sure." Remy rubs her nose and touches her hair and shoots a red-faced glance at me.

"Good night, kid," I say, snaking my finger up Remy's back as we hear Fry's footsteps go up the stairs and then move along the hallway above us.

A door slams and the TV blares, and we turn to each other and explode with mortified laughter. And now we're kissing, laughing, kissing again and laughing again, tasting each other and touching each other. I'm aching for her hands on my cock again, but although it was strangely arousing to almost get caught by the kid, now that he's in the house we can't risk it. Showing affection in front of a kid is one thing. Seeing his mom legs-up and naked on the kitchen island with my face buried in her muff, my cock bouncing and dripping all over, balls swinging like church bells . . . yeah, that might be a smidgeon past "healthy display of affection."

And so reluctantly I pull back from her and she nods and sighs. I cup her cheek and kiss her gently on the lips, and I see her pleading with those brown eyes.

"My study," she says. "It's soundproof. I had panels put in so I could do conference calls on speaker."

My cock moves like a dog straining at the leash, but I hold back the hounds and shake my head that's filling with images of making Remy scream as I spank her ass red and fuck her pussy pink. But if she and I are going to be something, then the rules need to be set early on. Especially with this woman. I can't forget that she's my match, a dominant woman who somehow gets me going in a way no submissive ever has.

"No." I pat my trousers and smile when I feel her damp panties in there. My trophy. A reminder of who's in control here. Her mouth hangs open and she straightens her back, her breasts sticking out in a way that makes me want to pant and howl and beg for it. But somehow I manage to get to the door. I stop, turn, and pull out those panties, holding them up to my face and sniffing like a filthy animal.

Remy makes a face and uncrosses her legs on that stool. I swallow hard when I see a shadowy glimpse of her naked pussy between those glistening thighs. I should leave but my feet are heavy like cinderblocks. I fist those panties and sniff them again, the blood rushing to my head and my cock at the same time. She knows what she's doing, and I know it too. This is a fucking showdown, a battle of wills, a test of who's going to lead and who will follow.

We watch each other like fighters before the bell. Then Remy puts her thighs together, slides off the stool, and shrugs before turning and strolling out of the floodlit kitchen, past the shadowy hall, and into the walnut paneled soundproof study. She kicks the door shut behind her, and I'm left staring at the dark wooden door, her flag in my hand, loaded gun in my pants.

And I growl when I realize what's happening.

She's going to make me knock.

She's going to make me beg.

She's going to make me break.

12

<u>REMY</u>

"**Y**ou'll have to break down this door to get in here."
I chuckle and then press my ear to the thick door.
It's soundproofed but there's a bit of space under
the door and around the hinges. I'd hear him knock.

So I wait. And I wait. But it feels awfully still
out there. Did Rhodes leave? Did he seriously
fucking *leave*?!

I wait a few more minutes, my heart sinking as
I step back from the door and walk to my big walnut wood desk. My thighs swish against each other, and it's so quiet in here I can almost hear my
pussy-lips squeak. Wait, what? Oh, right. Principal
Rhodes has my panties.

The grandfather clock in the corner ticks louder than I ever remember, and I sink into my swivel chair and rock back and forth. The chair squeaks too, and I frown when I realize that hell, there are a crapload of little sounds that I never noticed. The gentle whir of the humidifier. The whispering whoosh of the air flowing through the vents. The spinning hard drive in my computer that's always on. The occasional groan of the floorboards settling. Why did I never notice these sounds before? Were they always there?

"Focus on your other senses." I close my eyes and repeat what Rhodes said to me before that mind-blowing massage. I didn't do it then. But I do it now, taking a moment to appreciate the tiniest sound and smell until I swear I can hear the rustle of the rose bushes outside the window, smell the petals that have tightened up for the night. Soon I'm lost in the loudness of what seemed like silence, and a strange peace comes over me.

It's only now that I remember the events of the evening, when a man was in my house, hand on my throat, hedge-trimmers raised like in a teen horror flick. I was scared then, but I'm not scared now. I'm not jumping at shadows or absentmindedly brushing my teeth without toothpaste. If anything, tonight's the most fun I've had in years. And that moment when Fry almost caught us? Ohmygod, I know it's awful to think this, but it felt like such a wholesome moment in a way, didn't it? Almost a . . . a *family* moment!

"I can't believe he left," I say, biting my lip as I try to make sense of it. I thought we were just playing around, but there's something deadly serious about the way Rhodes plays. Like that stuff about not telling him what to do . . . shit, that wasn't play. That was real. He's for real, Remy. You sure you can handle a relationship with a man that dominant? What happens when two dominant people try to make a life together? Can it ever work?

I stroll to the window, where my roses bushes are moving gently in the night breeze. I glance past the leaves and buds to the street, and my heart skips when I see Rhodes's black pickup truck still parked out there!

Immediately I run to the door, leaning close and listening. Nothing. Do I dare open the door? Will I lose this little game if I let him in? Do I care?

I hold my breath and turn the knob, biting my lip as I feel the cool hallway air rush in. I peek through the crack, but there's no movement, no sound, and no man. I sigh and walk back to the window, and now my heart stumbles when I see the truck's got its interior lights on. I see Rhodes's big head with that hair thick like a bearskin rug. I'm sick to my stomach, but I keep watching, waiting for him to drive away, send me a clear message that even with a hard cock and heavy balls he's in control.

"Fuck you," I say. "Drive away. Leave. Go on. Get outta here. Go. Just *go!*"

But he doesn't go.

He stays.

In his truck.

Keeping watch.

You're safe, Rhodes had said. *Fry is safe. You're safe. You'll always be safe.*

And now I see the real message. That although Rhodes will walk away to send me a message that he's in charge, he'll never walk away from something that's not a game.

"I'm here to stay. That's what he's saying. That's his message," I whisper, placing my hand on the cool window glass as a warm tear rolls down my left cheek. "I'm here to stay."

Stay forever.

13
<u>THE NEXT DAY</u>
<u>RHODES</u>

"You have an appointment?" I smile as Remy pokes her head around the half-open door to my office.

"I do, actually." She steps in and closes the door behind her. "I believe you have something of mine."

I reach for the top left drawer in my desk and pull it open. I glance down and grunt. "I claimed them. And I'm keeping them. Anything else on the agenda for this meeting?"

Remy smiles and steps close to the desk. She's dressed in a black suit today, looking sexy as sin in black heels and a black tank-top that reminds me I still haven't sucked those nipples. Fuck, this morning was torture getting my pants on over the hard-on that kept me up in the truck all fucking night.

But it was worth it, I think as I remember seeing her at the window. Worth it to send her a message that I know hit home, showed her that it *does* mean something to have a man around the house, that relying on a man doesn't make you less capable or less powerful or less awesome as a Mom.

"Sit." I slide the drawer shut and place my palms flat on the desk. I wait for her to sit. She does it. I smile. Then I lose the smile and watch her shift her ass on the chair. I know she's got an agenda in her head. An agenda I have no intention of following.

"I want to discuss last night," she says firmly, fixing her gaze on me like I bet she does at business meetings. Won't work, because this isn't a fucking business meeting. This is personal.

"There will be no discussion." I dig my elbows into the desk and tent my fingers below my chin. "Just a statement of decision. My decision."

She blinks and quickly glances down at the desk. Then she looks back into my eyes and I see her throat move as she swallows. Immediately I know I got to her last night by walking away but also staying. It got her all turned around. She knows I can resist that sweet pussy even when it's close enough to taste. But at the same time, she knows I'm here to stay.

Stay forever.

"What decision?" she says, trying to be stoic but failing in the most delightful way.

"I never want to find out," I say.

She swallows, her eyes telling me she knows what I mean. She nods and swallows again, turning her head and touching the corner of her eye. "I don't either," she says softly, dabbing her eye again and smiling hesitantly at me.

"Good." I feel a lump in my throat but manage to keep my voice steady. "There's something else. Another decision."

"Now what?" she says, trying to roll her shining eyes but not pulling it off.

I pull open that drawer and glance down and then back at her. "I said I'm keeping these. But that's not the only thing I'm keeping." I slam the drawer shut and make her jump. "I'm keeping you too," I whisper. "I'm keeping you too, Remy."

14
<u>THREE MONTHS LATER</u>
<u>REMY</u>

"Can we keep her, Mom? Please? *Please*?!"

I sigh and shake my head as Fry holds up a snow-white kitten with an adorable black spot over its left eye—its *green* left eye. I glance over at Rhodes, who's in his new tailored navy suit that I insisted he get. He's over with the folks from the animal shelter who are running their event where they bring over puppies and kittens from the shelter and supervise the kids as they interact with the fluffy critters. All the kids need to have a parent with them for liability purposes, which is why I'm skipping work to get white fur on my black skirt.

"I told you, Fry," I say. "These animals are just here for the event. We can't adopt any of them. Right, Principal Rhodes?" I wink up at Rhodes as he strolls over, hands in his trouser pockets. The school knows we're a couple now, and although tongues wagged worse than puppy-tails at play-time, the rumors died down when it became clear we weren't violating any policy and Fry wasn't getting any special treatment.

Of course, one of the rumors that spread was about Fry. The teachers noticed the green eyes, and although Fry's provenance isn't part of the school records, the staff have never heard me talk of Fry's dad. So naturally the little gossips wondered if Rhodes and I have a secret past.

Which we do, of course. The twist is it was a secret from *both* of us.

And it'll always be a secret, I think as I smile at my son and then look up at the man Fry's already aching to call Dad. Aching in a way that tugs at my heart.

"Can we?" he says to Rhodes, looking up at him like they really are father and son.

Rhodes glances down at him, looks over at me, and then shrugs. "Yes. Go ahead. I'll take care of the paperwork."

I stare open-mouthed as Fry scoops up the kitten and runs off to tell his friends. My hands go to my hips and my gaze to his smug face. "What was that?"

"A decision," he grunts. "Gotta make them quick and loose. Shoot from the hip."

I snort and glance down at his muscular hips. "I guess I can't argue with that. One shot from your hip got me the best darned green-eyed kid in the world."

Rhodes chuckles and pulls me in for a quick hug. I squeeze his arm and then break away when I see his assistant hurrying over, adjusting her glasses and clearing her throat. Rhodes steps away to talk to her, and I go over to where Fry's got that kitten doing jumping jacks on a tiny cat-trampoline.

I watch the kids laugh and squeal, and I think back to that whole shooting from the hip thing. In three months together we made it a point to never talk about that, to never lose sight that this is about us and nothing else, that if we're married Fry will be Rhodes's son and we don't need a DNA test to tell us what we feel in our hearts. What we'll *always* feel in our hearts, no matter what that test might say.

I turn to see if Rhodes is done with his assistant, but he's nowhere to be seen. Strange. He usually prioritizes events with parents and staff. I wonder what's up.

Soon the event wraps up, and once I assure Fry his kitten will be waiting for him at home later, I take the stairs up to the third floor to see if Rhodes is in his office.

When I get to the waiting room, I see a woman in a blue skirt-suit sitting quietly with a little girl I assume is her daughter. I smile at the woman. She smiles back, but it's forced, like her mind is elsewhere. I figure she's got an appointment with Rhodes, but I wonder why she's stressed.

Now the daughter looks up at me and I smile down at her.

But my face freezes mid-smile when I look into the little girl's eyes.

The little girl's *green* eyes!

I stumble backwards, my airways closing up as I image a million little Rhodes' popping up everywhere, a million women laying claim to my man even though I know the idea is ridiculous.

In fact the idea is impossible.

Because I paid the La Jolla center a extra fee for exclusive rights to the seed I selected. And since Rhodes assured me that he'd only done it once, and only at La Jolla, I rested easy knowing Fry didn't have any half-siblings floating around out there.

But now I'm wondering if Rhodes was being truthful.

And the more I look at the little girl, the more I wonder.

I wonder until I can't help myself. And finally I smile sweetly at the little girl and say, "You here alone with your Mom, sweetie? Daddy couldn't get off from work?"

The girl shakes her head. Then she points all her fingers at the door to Rhodes's office. "My Daddy's in there."

A chill goes through me as I glance at the door. I shake my head as if to clear it, but it's only getting foggier. I don't know exactly what I'm feeling, but it's not good, and I bite my lip and try to push away the thoughts swarming through my head like a pit of snakes.

"Here he is! Daddy! Daddy!" cries the little girl, and I turn as the door opens and Rhodes steps out, a big grin on his lying face! The girl rushes towards him, and I'm about to rush out the other way, out of this drama, out of this dream, out of this nightmare.

But then the girl races past Rhodes, and I almost faint when I see another man walk out of the office. He picks up the little girl and plants a big kiss on her forehead, his beaming smile crinkling up his warm eyes.

Warm green eyes.

Green like his daughter's eyes.

Green like my shame, my possessiveness, my need to have all of Rhodes, control all of him, keep all of him to myself.

When I regain control the waiting room is empty except for me and Rhodes. He's got a strange look on his face, his large body taking up most of the space in the doorway to his office. One look into those green eyes and I know he's figured out where my mind just went, and I shrug my guilty red face and bite my lip hard in the hopes that I can chew through my shame.

"Ms. Remy. In my office, please. Now." Rhodes strokes his beard and holds the door wide for me. I nod and walk in with my eyes averted, legs together, hands folded at my front.

"It's not what it looked like," I say, my face burning with the memory of where my thoughts took me. "I never doubted you, Rhodes. I swear it."

"Swearing isn't tolerated in this school." Rhodes has his back to me. He's doing something on his desk. "Come on. Up. It's time, Remy. I held off for three months because you've been good. But there's no more holding back. I know what you were thinking when you saw that girl, and if you were thinking what I thought you were thinking, it means you believe that I lied to you about where I spread my studly seed. If you think I lied to you, it means you doubted me. Doubt on the battlefield gets people killed."

"Well, this isn't a battlefield," I say.

"Marriage is always a battlefield."

"We aren't married."

"We will be soon."

I raise an eyebrow. "Is that a proposal?"

Rhodes grunts. "A proposal is a question, and I don't ask questions. I make decisions, and this one got made three months ago."

"That's news to me."

He frowns. "Didn't I tell you I was keeping you?"

I widen my mouth in an over-the-top O. "*That* was your marriage proposal?"

"Told you. Decision, not proposal. Now come on. No stalling. It's time. Up you go."

I barely hear him, I'm so giddy with the sudden switch from being sure this was a mistake ten minutes ago to facing the simple truth that he's already decided to marry me, to make me his, to keep me forever like I'm being captured and put in a drawer along with my panties.

"It's time? Time for what?" I say, my frazzled brain finally letting his words through.

But Rhodes doesn't answer. Instead he steps

aside to reveal his desk cleared down to the last pencil. Nothing but smooth tabletop. He pats it gently, his expression far from gentle. Then I notice something in his other hand, and I gasp when I see it's a long, thick, flat wooden ruler, old-school and heavy, the wood dark and smooth with age.

"Time for what?" I whisper, my panties getting sucked into my clenching pussy when I see the look in his eyes.

He pats the tabletop again, this time with the ruler. "Time to be punished," he growls. "Punished by the Principal."

I stare long and hard, wondering if this man is serious. He returns my stare with a gaze that's longer and harder, and I've got my answer. I glance at the smooth table, then at the rough ruler, finally at those green eyes shining from a savage bearded face.

"Marriage is a battlefield," I mutter as I feel my big butt tighten in anticipation. "So I'll surrender this battle . . . surrender because I've already won the war."

And so I wobble on one heel and remove my panties and hand them over as the spoils to the victor. Then I hike up my skirt, clamber on the desk with my heels on, and raise my rump for the stern discipline of the Principal.

15
<u>RHODES</u>

It's good to be the Principal.

Her ass is so smooth and round and perfect that
I stand there drooling and panting, my cock harder
than the wooden ruler that's cutting into my palms
from my viselike grip. Slowly I trace the edge of the
ruler around each buttcheek, delighting in how

Remy tightens up, how those prickly goosebumps pop up in lines following the path of my ruler.

"Oh, shit, Rhodes," she groans as I tease her long dark rear crack with the edge of the ruler, parting those cheeks and almost collapsing when I catch a glimpse of that perfect little pucker, clean and shiny like a full moon eclipse. "What are you doing to me?"

I take a growling breath as I take another long look at her asshole before letting her bountiful buttocks hide her secret from my hungry gaze. "I should ask you the same thing," I mutter. "Sure as hell feels like you're in control more than I am."

Remy giggles, her laughter thick in her throat. "I don't think either of us is in control."

"Huh," I grunt, stroking my chin. "Maybe that's the only way we get peace in our battlefield of a marriage. If we're *both* out of control."

"You're a delusional idiot if you believe that— *OW! Ohmygod, did you just . . . OW!*"

I bring the ruler down firmly across her ass, the smooth flatness of the ruler sending a dull *thwack* through the closed room, the sound ricocheting off the walls as Remy's ass trembles and her fingers claw at the desk. Her face is red from the shock, and I give her a moment and then plant three more swift strikes on the meatiest part of her bum.

She cries out again, and now I'm losing control. I toss the ruler away and jam my face between those cheeks, driving my tongue past her dark rim and sliding my fingers into her cunt from below. She gushes all over my hand until her wetness drips onto my school-issued desk, but I'm so far gone I don't give a fuck.

I tongue-fuck her asshole like the filthy green-eyed monster I am, and then I pull back and spank her twice on each buttcheek, growling again as I see my paw marks on her smooth round ass. One last smack and then I finger her rear hole while furiously unbuckling and unzipping. I'm on the desk before my pants are all the way off, and I'm inside her so deep she gurgles like she feels it in her throat.

She comes all over my shaft and balls as I ram her deep, two fingers plunged in her asshole, curled up so I can control that squirming hourglass of a body. I claw at her boobs through her tank-top, pinching her nipples so hard she jerks back and screams.

I shout out too as I thrust back into her. Thankfully my assistant is on her lunch break, but I doubt I'd have stopped if she were outside. Nah, I wouldn't have stopped.

Because I know what I've always known: That

once you cross a line in battle there's no turning back. You just face forward and keep going. Play for keeps.

And this is for keeps, I think as I feel my body tighten, my cock flex, my throat close as my balls serve up my seed in a massive explosion that would have won all of America's wars with one shot of hot seed.

Seed that found its way home ten years ago, and is finding its way home again.

Just like I've found my way home.

Found my woman.

Found my family.

Found my always.

And my forever.

∞

EPILOGUE
<u>ELEVEN YEARS LATER</u>
<u>REMY</u>

"Happy twenty-first birthday, Fry!" I say before smothering my grown-up little man with a big, wet, proud kiss. Rhodes has the camera going, and all five of our kids are clawing at the cake like we're still living in caves.

"Randy and Racer!" Rhodes shouts to the seven-year-old twins. "And hey, Rhonda, Relsie, Raya—please at least *pretend* to use a plate, yeah?"

Our four-year-old triplets wave off the big bad Principal, and I hug Fry once more as Rhodes strolls over. He's got a white envelope in his right hand, and I feel a chill go through my spine. I know what's in that envelope. Both Rhodes and I know.

Well, that's not quite true. We know what's in it. But we also *don't* know what's in it.

Because we kept our promises to each other. We never want to know. But we decided that maybe Fry would like to know who his biological father is—if the man he's called Dad for a decade really is Dad.

"What's this?" Fry says, licking some cake off his thumb and frowning at the envelope. "Money?" he asks with a wink.

Rhodes snorts. Then he pulls Fry aside and I touch my hair and watch my son's expression. Fry shoots a look at me, his face flushed as he turns over the envelope and studies the seal. I know Rhodes told him that we don't know and we don't want to know because it won't change how we feel. But we want him to have the choice. To make the choice himself.

Fry holds that sealed envelope in his hand through the duration of our little family party. Then as the younger kids drop out for the TV and video games, taking the slow-walking Dog and the still-spry Cat with them, Fry sighs and looks warmly at each of us.

"I love you, Mom," he says. Then he takes a long look at Rhodes, who's strangely tight. "And I fucking love you . . . Dad. *Dad*. You hear that? Dad. Dad. *Dad*!"

And as we watch, Fry reaches for a solitary unburned candle. He places it on a small triangle of birthday cake that's left on the plate. He lights the candle with the red kitchen lighter.

Then, his green eyes focused on the two of us, he holds that still-sealed envelope over the open flame.

∞

FROM THE AUTHOR

Thanks for reading!
Hope you liked that one!

The CURVY FOR KEEPS Series screams on with
another over-the-top rager: STRANDED WITH
THE PSYCHO!

If you want more wildness, catch up with some
of my other super-hot stuff: DRAGON'S CURVY
MATE and CURVY FOR HIM!

Also, if you like college romances (Annabelle
Winters style, of course . . .) try the CURVY IN
COLLEGE Series!

Thanks and Love,
Anna.

∞

Books by Annabelle Winters

The CURVES FOR SHEIKHS Series

Curves for the Sheikh
Flames for the Sheikh
Hostage for the Sheikh
Single for the Sheikh
Stockings for the Sheikh
Untouched for the Sheikh
Surrogate for the Sheikh
Stars for the Sheikh
Shelter for the Sheikh
Shared for the Sheikh
Assassin for the Sheikh
Privilege for the Sheikh
Ransomed for the Sheikh
Uncorked for the Sheikh
Haunted for the Sheikh
Grateful for the Sheikh
Mistletoe for the Sheikh
Fake for the Sheikh

The CURVES FOR SHIFTERS Series

Curves for the Dragon
Born for the Bear
Witch for the Wolf
Tamed for the Lion
Taken for the Tiger

The CURVY FOR HIM Series

The Teacher and the Trainer
The Librarian and the Cop
The Lawyer and the Cowboy
The Princess and the Pirate

The CEO and the Soldier
The Astronaut and the Alien
The Botanist and the Biker
The Psychic and the Senator

THE CURVY FOR THE HOLIDAYS SERIES
Taken on Thanksgiving
Captive for Christmas
Night Before New Year's
Vampire's Curvy Valentine
Flagged on the Fourth
Home for Halloween

THE CURVY FOR KEEPS SERIES
Summoned by the CEO
Given to the Groom

THE DRAGON'S CURVY MATE SERIES
Dragon's Curvy Assistant
Dragon's Curvy Banker
Dragon's Curvy Counselor
Dragon's Curvy Doctor
Dragon's Curvy Engineer
Dragon's Curvy Firefighter
Dragon's Curvy Gambler

THE CURVY IN COLLEGE SERIES
The Jock and the Genius
The Rockstar and the Recluse
The Dropout and the Debutante
The Player and the Princess
The Fratboy and the Feminist

WWW.ANNABELLEWINTERS.

Made in the USA
Coppell, TX
06 April 2022

76116456R10069